Lerner SPORTS

GREATEST OF ALL TIME TEAMS

G.O.A.T.
BASEBALL TEAMS

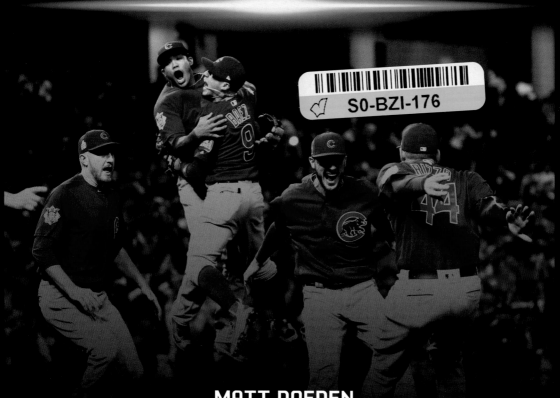

SO-BZI-176

MATT DOEDEN

Lerner Publications ◆ Minneapolis

Lerner Publications Company
An imprint of Lerner Publishing Group, Inc.
241 First Avenue North
Minneapolis, MN 55401 USA

For reading levels and more information, look up this title at www.lernerbooks.com.

Main body text set in Aptifer Sans LT Pro. Typeface provided by Linotype AG.

Editor: Shee Yang
Lerner team: Martha Kranes

Library of Congress Cataloging-in-Publication Data

Names: Doeden, Matt, author.
Title: G.O.A.T. baseball teams / Matt Doeden.
Description: Minneapolis : Lerner Publications Group, Inc, [2021] | Series: Greatest of all time teams (Lerner sports) | Includes bibliographical references and index. | Audience: Ages 7–11 | Audience: Grades 2–3 | Summary: "Which baseball teams are the greatest of all time? From the 2005 Chicago White Sox to the 1942 St. Louis Cardinals, find out which teams make the cut in this easy-to-follow ranking"— Provided by publisher.
Identifiers: LCCN 2020009433 (print) | LCCN 2020009434 (ebook) | ISBN 9781728404417 (library binding) | ISBN 9781728418223 (ebook)
Subjects: LCSH: Baseball teams—United States—Juvenile literature. | Major League Baseball (Organization)—Juvenile literature.
Classification: LCC GV875.A1 D628 2021 (print) | LCC GV875.A1 (ebook) | DDC 796.357/640973—dc23

LC record available at https://lccn.loc.gov/2020009433
LC ebook record available at https://lccn.loc.gov/2020009434

Manufactured in the United States of America.
1-48499-49013-7/7/2020

TABLE OF CONTENTS

PLAY BALL! — 4

NO. 10 2005 CHICAGO WHITE SOX — 8

NO. 9 2001 SEATTLE MARINERS — 10

NO. 8 1976 CINCINNATI REDS — 12

NO. 7 1970 BALTIMORE ORIOLES — 14

NO. 6 2016 CHICAGO CUBS — 16

NO. 5 1998 NEW YORK YANKEES — 18

NO. 4 1942 ST. LOUIS CARDINALS — 20

NO. 3 1939 NEW YORK YANKEES — 22

NO. 2 1929 PHILADELPHIA ATHLETICS — 24

NO. 1 1927 NEW YORK YANKEES — 26

YOUR G.O.A.T. — 28
BASEBALL FACTS — 29
GLOSSARY — 30
LEARN MORE — 31
INDEX — 32

The Commissioner's Trophy is awarded to the World Series champions each year.

PLAY BALL!

For more than a century, baseball fans have argued about which team is the greatest of all time (G.O.A.T.). The champions of the American League (AL) and National League (NL) meet in the World Series to crown a season champion. But what about comparing teams from different years and different eras?

ENTED BY THE COMMISSIONER OF BASEBALL

FACTS AT A GLANCE

>> The 2001 Seattle Mariners won a record 116 games, but they failed to reach the World Series.

>> The Cincinnati Reds were 7–0 in the 1976 postseason, making them the only playoff-era team to go undefeated.

>> The Chicago Cubs won the World Series in 2016, the team's first championship in 108 years.

>> The 1998 New York Yankees won 125 games combined in the regular season and postseason, the most of any championship team.

>> In 1927, the Yankees won the AL by a whopping 19 games over the Philadelphia Athletics.

The basics of baseball haven't changed much since the first World Series in 1902. But the way the game is played has changed a lot. Baseball players are bigger and stronger than in the past. They have access to medical experts, money, and unlimited information. A century ago, none of that was true. Many big leaguers needed to find work during the off-season to make ends meet.

Before 1947, Major League Baseball (MLB) was a segregated game. Players of color were banned from playing. Once Jackie Robinson joined the Brooklyn Dodgers in 1947,

Jackie Robinson pictured (*right*) with Dodgers teammates (*from left to right*) Johnny Jorgensen, Pee Wee Reese, and Eddie Stanky

Robinson played his first MLB game 17 years before the US Civil Rights Act ended segregation in public places in 1964.

everything changed. A new wave of stars such as Willie Mays and Hank Aaron became the new faces of the game.

Fans have to weigh all of these factors as they choose the G.O.A.T. team. As you read about the teams in this book, you'll form your own opinions. What do you value most in a great team? How do you compare a team from the 1920s to a team from the 2020s? What defines greatness to you?

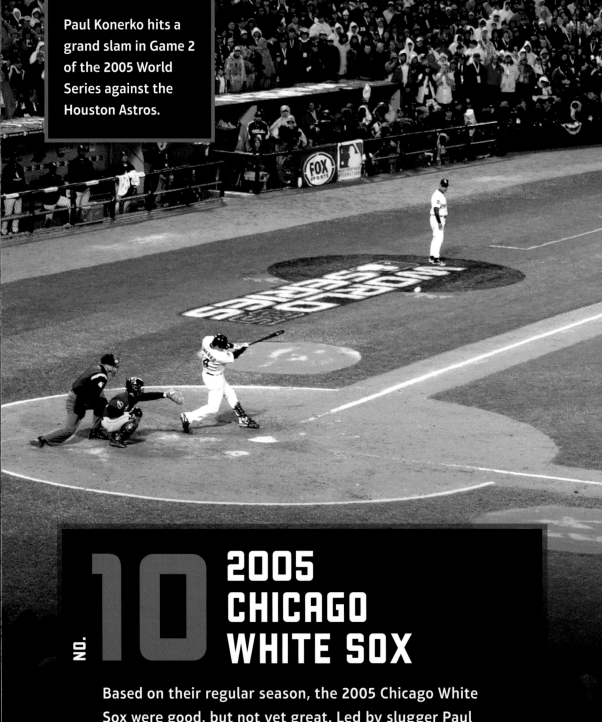

Paul Konerko hits a grand slam in Game 2 of the 2005 World Series against the Houston Astros.

NO. 10

2005 CHICAGO WHITE SOX

Based on their regular season, the 2005 Chicago White Sox were good, but not yet great. Led by slugger Paul Konerko and ace Mark Buehrle, they won 99 games and claimed the AL Central crown.

Then came the playoffs, and good became great. The White Sox opened the first round with a 14–2 win, bumping off the Boston Red Sox. They went on to sweep Boston 3–0 in the series to advance to the American League Championship Series (ALCS).

The wins kept coming. They beat the Los Angeles Angels of Anaheim 4–1 in the ALCS and then swept the Houston Astros in the World Series. Their postseason record was stunning—11 wins and just a single loss. The White Sox outscored their opponents by a total of 33 runs. And they made their mark as one of the greatest postseason teams in baseball history.

Mark Buehrle

2005 WHITE SOX STATS

>>> Chicago went 11–1 in the postseason to win the World Series.

>>> They won 99 games during the regular season.

>>> The White Sox claimed their first World Series title in 88 years.

>>> The White Sox went 52–29 in games away from Chicago.

>>> First baseman Paul Konerko hit 40 home runs and drove in 100 runs.

Ichiro Suzuki gets ready to swing during a game on April 18, 2001.

NO. 9 2001 SEATTLE MARINERS

In 2001, speedy outfielder Ichiro Suzuki left Japan to join the Seattle Mariners. His arrival marked the beginning of an amazing year. In his first big-league season, Suzuki collected 242 hits, batted .350, and won both the AL's Rookie of the Year and Most Valuable

Freddy Garcia pitches the ball during a 7–5 victory against the Toronto Blue Jays.

The Mariners built a strong lineup and solid pitching staff around their new star. Led by starters Freddy Garcia and Jamie Moyer, the team finished the month of April with a record of 20–5 and never looked back. On October 6, the Mariners won their 116th game, setting a major-league record.

But as great as the regular season was, the Mariners didn't make it to the World Series. They lost to the New York Yankees in the ALCS. Many call them the best baseball team not to win the championship.

2001 MARINERS STATS

▶▶▶ Seattle went 116–46 in the regular season to tie a record for the most wins.

▶▶▶ Seattle won 59 games by four runs or more, an MLB record.

▶▶▶ Suzuki collected 242 hits and won both MVP and Rookie of the Year honors.

▶▶▶ Seattle won 15 games in a row from May 23 to June 8, 2001.

▶▶▶ The Mariners lost to the Yankees in the ALCS 4–1.

Cesar Geronimo slides home in Game 2 of the 1976 World Series against the New York Yankees.

NO. 8

1976 CINCINNATI REDS

In the mid-1970s, the Cincinnati Reds were known as the Big Red Machine. The machine was never more finely tuned than in 1976. A star-studded lineup featured seven NL All-Stars, including Johnny Bench, Pete Rose, Joe Morgan, and George Foster. The Reds outscored every other team in baseball by more than 100 runs!

The Sporting News

OCTOBER 23, 1976   Price: 75 Cents

REDS' MUSCLEMEN

The Reds appeared on the cover of the *Sporting News* in 1976.

The Reds cruised to the NL East title with 102 wins, the most in baseball that year. Then they got even better. Cincinnati tore through the playoffs without losing a single game, a feat no other team has ever accomplished. They capped off their amazing season by outscoring the New York Yankees in the World Series, 22–8 over four games. Their perfect postseason cemented their place as one of baseball's G.O.A.T. teams.

1976 REDS STATS

- The Reds went 53–28 in games away from Cincinnati.

- Joe Morgan batted .320, slugged 27 home runs, and was named NL MVP.

- Cincinnati scored 857 runs, 87 more than the Philadelphia Phillies, who finished second with 770.

- The Reds won the NL West division by 10 games over the Los Angeles Dodgers.

- Johnny Bench batted .533 and hit two home runs in the World Series. He was named World Series MVP.

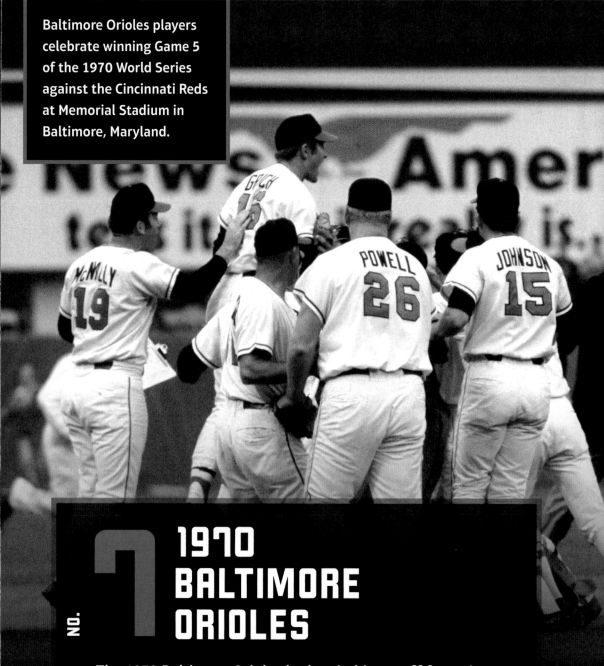

Baltimore Orioles players celebrate winning Game 5 of the 1970 World Series against the Cincinnati Reds at Memorial Stadium in Baltimore, Maryland.

1970 BALTIMORE ORIOLES

The 1970 Baltimore Orioles had a pitching staff featuring superstars Jim Palmer, Dave McNally, and Mike Cuellar. Their lineup was anchored by third baseman Boog Powell, who hit 35 home runs on his way to winning AL MVP honors.

The Orioles crushed the AL East in the regular season, winning 108 games and beating the second-place Yankees by a stunning 15 games. From there, they dominated the postseason. They swept the Twins in the ALCS and then beat the Reds 4–1 in the World Series. Along the way, they scored 60 runs in just eight postseason games.

Boog Powell

1970 ORIOLES STATS

- ▶▶▶ Baltimore had a winning streak of 11 games from September 20 to October 1.

- ▶▶▶ The Orioles never lost more than three games in a row all season.

- ▶▶▶ They won the AL East by 15 games over the New York Yankees.

- ▶▶▶ They outscored their opponents 60–29 in the postseason.

- ▶▶▶ Brooks Robinson batted .429 in the World Series. He also hit two home runs and earned World Series MVP honors.

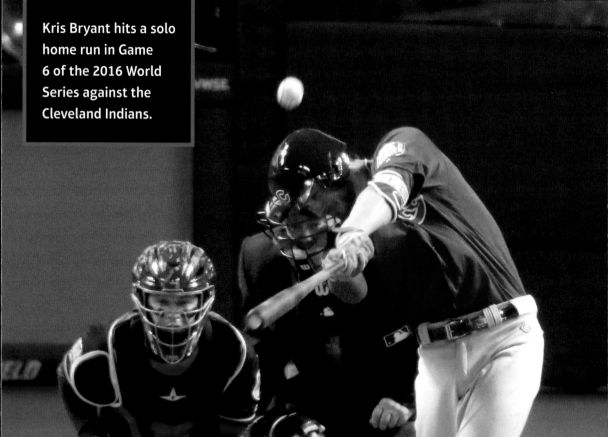

Kris Bryant hits a solo home run in Game 6 of the 2016 World Series against the Cleveland Indians.

6

2016 CHICAGO CUBS

Before the 2016 season, many Cubs fans were convinced that the team was cursed. Chicago hadn't won a World Series in 108 years. But the 2016 Cubs finally broke that curse. They did it behind slugging third baseman Kris Bryant, who belted 39 home runs in the regular season.

Members of the Cubs celebrate defeating the Cleveland Indians in Game 7 of the 2016 World Series.

The Cubs had 103 regular-season wins, the most that year. They beat the San Francisco Giants and Los Angeles Dodgers in the playoffs to advance to one of the most thrilling World Series of all time. After trailing Cleveland 3–1, the Cubs stormed back to force a deciding Game 7. It was tied 6–6 at the end of nine innings. In the 10th inning, Chicago's Ben Zobrist smacked a double to drive in a run and end the curse once and for all.

2016 CUBS STATS

- ▶▶▶ The Cubs went 17–6 in April.
- ▶▶▶ Chicago led the major leagues with 103 wins in the regular season.
- ▶▶▶ Third baseman Kris Bryant led the team with 39 home runs.
- ▶▶▶ The Cubs went 57–24 in home games.
- ▶▶▶ The Cubs won the NL Central by 17.5 games.
- ▶▶▶ They won the team's first World Series title since 1908, a span of 108 seasons.

Yankees closer Mariano Rivera in 1998 in a game against the Minnesota Twins

NO. 5

1998 NEW YORK YANKEES

Few teams have dominated baseball the way the Yankees did in 1998. Shortstop Derek Jeter was the spark plug for an offense that scored a league-high 965 runs. Starting pitchers David Cone and David Wells anchored the starting rotation. Closer Mariano Rivera was almost untouchable, saving 36 games with a low earned run average (ERA) of 1.91.

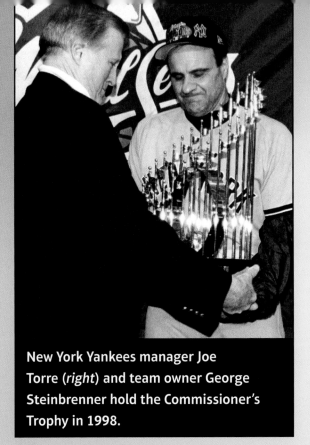

New York Yankees manager Joe Torre (*right*) and team owner George Steinbrenner hold the Commissioner's Trophy in 1998.

The Yankees blew the AL East away during the regular season, beating the second-place Boston Red Sox by 22 games. Then they crushed all four opponents in the postseason, going 11–2 on their way to the team's 24th World Series title. Their 125 combined wins remains the most ever for a championship team.

The Yankees won four World Series in five seasons from 1996 to 2000, and 1998 was the high point of one of the few dynasties in recent baseball history.

1998 YANKEES STATS

- The Yankees won 125 games between the regular season and postseason, the most ever by a championship team.

- Bernie Williams won the AL batting title with a .339 batting average.

- New York went 62–19 at home during the regular season.

- They won 10 games in a row between June 30 and July 12.

- New York swept the San Diego Padres in the World Series.

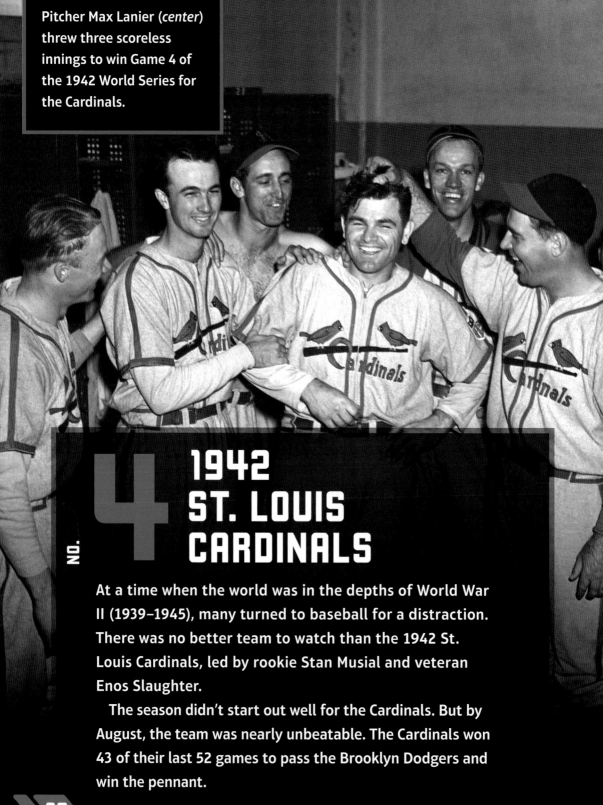

Pitcher Max Lanier (*center*) threw three scoreless innings to win Game 4 of the 1942 World Series for the Cardinals.

NO. 4

1942 ST. LOUIS CARDINALS

At a time when the world was in the depths of World War II (1939–1945), many turned to baseball for a distraction. There was no better team to watch than the 1942 St. Louis Cardinals, led by rookie Stan Musial and veteran Enos Slaughter.

The season didn't start out well for the Cardinals. But by August, the team was nearly unbeatable. The Cardinals won 43 of their last 52 games to pass the Brooklyn Dodgers and win the pennant.

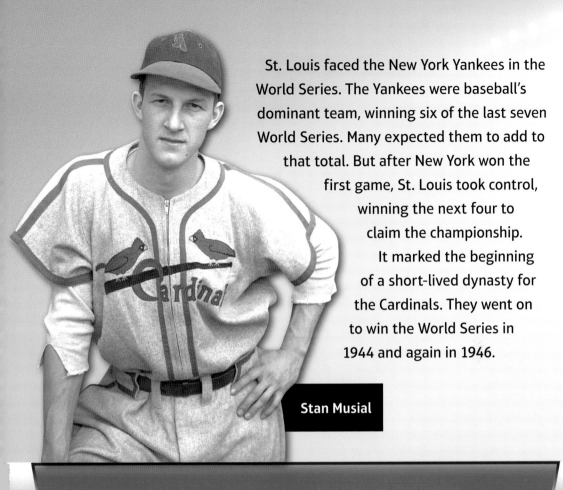

St. Louis faced the New York Yankees in the World Series. The Yankees were baseball's dominant team, winning six of the last seven World Series. Many expected them to add to that total. But after New York won the first game, St. Louis took control, winning the next four to claim the championship. It marked the beginning of a short-lived dynasty for the Cardinals. They went on to win the World Series in 1944 and again in 1946.

Stan Musial

1942 CARDINALS STATS

>>> The Cardinals went 60–17 at home during the regular season.

>>> Pitcher Mort Cooper went 22–7 and was named NL MVP.

>>> Stan Musial, just 21, batted .315 in his rookie season.

>>> The Cardinals were a young team, with 30-year-old outfielder Terry Moore as their oldest player.

>>> The Cardinals won the first of three World Series titles in five seasons (1942, 1944, 1946).

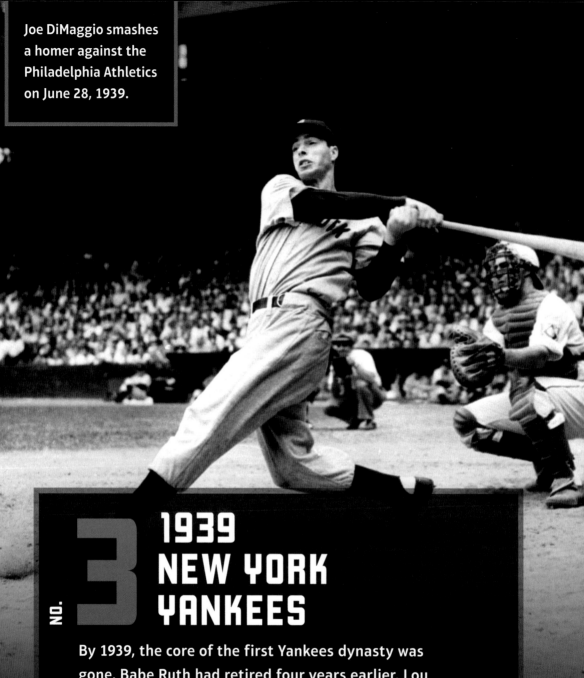

NO. 3
1939 NEW YORK YANKEES

By 1939, the core of the first Yankees dynasty was gone. Babe Ruth had retired four years earlier. Lou Gehrig was forced out of the game in June 1939 due to a deadly disease.

But a new star, 24-year-old Joe DiMaggio, was rising to take their place. Joltin' Joe was a hitting machine. He batted .389 in the season with 30 home runs. And the Yankees

New York Yankees outfielders Charlie Keller (*left*) and Joe DiMaggio pictured together in 1939

didn't miss a beat. They won 106 games in the regular season. They didn't spend a single day out of first place.

The Yankees faced the Cincinnati Reds in the World Series. It was no contest. Outfielder Charlie Keller was the star of the series, batting .438 with three home runs in the four-game sweep. Despite the loss of several of the biggest stars in MLB history, the Yankees' dominance of the AL was far from over.

1939 YANKEES STATS

- ▶▶▶ The Yankees went 106–45 in the regular season.
- ▶▶▶ The Yankees won the AL by 17 games over the Red Sox.
- ▶▶▶ New York scored 23 runs in a single game on June 28.
- ▶▶▶ They outscored their opponents by 411 runs during the regular season.
- ▶▶▶ The Yankees shut out their opponents 15 times and were shut out just once.

NO. 2

1929 PHILADELPHIA ATHLETICS

The Philadelphia Athletics looked like a clear second-place team at the start of the season. The Yankees were in the midst of a dynasty, and it didn't feel as if anyone in the AL could stop them.

Yet that's what the Athletics did. Outfielder Al Simmons and first baseman Jimmie Foxx were hitting machines. But the team was really built on pitching. The Philadelphia staff, led by 20-game-winner Lefty Grove, posted an ERA of 3.44, more than half a run lower than any other team in the league. Even the

Robert Moses "Lefty" Grove in 1929

Yankees were no match. The Athletics won the pennant by a whopping 18 games.

Their greatness carried into the World Series. The Athletics beat the Cubs in five games, including an amazing comeback in Game 4. The Athletics trailed Chicago 8–0 in the seventh inning and then scored 10 runs to steal the victory. When it was all over, few could deny it was one of the greatest seasons in baseball history.

1929 ATHLETICS STATS

>>> Lefty Grove led the AL in both ERA (2.81) and strikeouts (170).

>>> Philadelphia outscored opponents 901–615 during the regular season.

>>> The Athletics scored 24 runs in a game on May 1.

>>> The Athletics had a record of 57–16 in home games.

>>> In the World Series, Jimmie Foxx batted .350 and slugged two home runs.

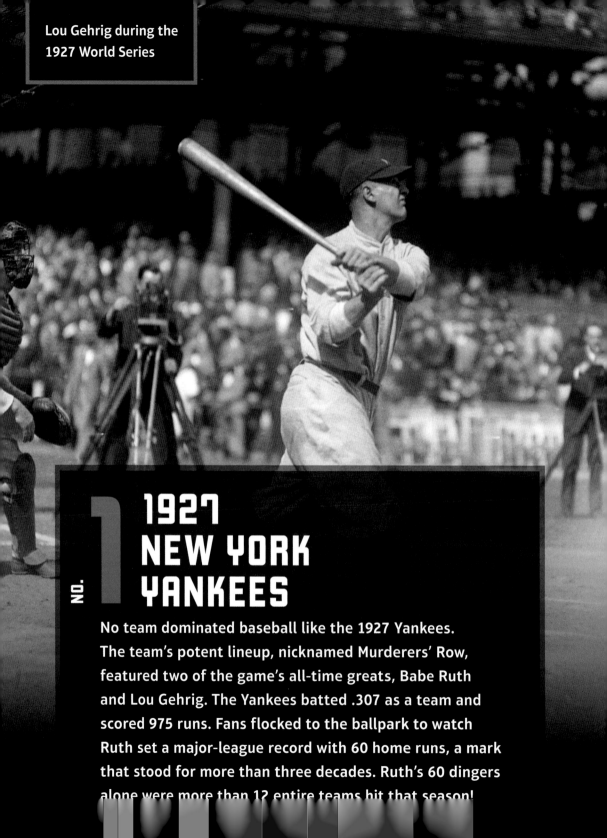

Lou Gehrig during the 1927 World Series

NO. 1

1927 NEW YORK YANKEES

No team dominated baseball like the 1927 Yankees. The team's potent lineup, nicknamed Murderers' Row, featured two of the game's all-time greats, Babe Ruth and Lou Gehrig. The Yankees batted .307 as a team and scored 975 runs. Fans flocked to the ballpark to watch Ruth set a major-league record with 60 home runs, a mark that stood for more than three decades. Ruth's 60 dingers alone were more than 12 entire teams hit that season!

Super sluggers Lou Gehrig (*left*) and Babe Ruth in 1927

And the pitching staff, led by Waite Hoyt, were just as good. They led the league with a team ERA of just 3.20.

The Yankees cruised to a 110–44 record, beating the Athletics for the pennant by 19 games. Then they swept the Pittsburgh Pirates in the World Series. Ruth was the hero, batting .400 in the series and belting two home runs. When it was all over, the Yankees stood alone as the greatest baseball team of all time.

1927 YANKEES STATS

>>> The Yankees never spent a single day out of first place.

>>> Lou Gehrig belted 47 home runs and was named AL MVP.

>>> The team's combined 114–44 record gave them a winning percentage of .721, the highest in baseball history.

>>> The Yankees won the AL by 19 games over the Athletics.

>>> New York led MLB in home runs (158), runs scored (976), and batting average (.307).

YOUR
G.O.A.T.

IT'S TIME TO MAKE YOUR OWN G.O.A.T. LIST.

Do you value championships above all else? Or does the regular season matter more to you? Make your own G.O.A.T. list. Check out other books on baseball's greatest teams. Look at stats and records on websites such as baseball-reference.com. Talk to fellow baseball fans, young and old, to get their opinions.

For fun, ask a friend or family member to make a list too. Then you can compare them. Which teams do you agree on? Where do you disagree? Discuss your lists and defend your choices. And the fun doesn't have to stop there. Make other top 10 lists. What are the greatest World Series of all time? Which are baseball's all-time worst teams? It's all up to you!

BASEBALL FACTS

>>> The New York Yankees have three times as many championships as their division rivals the Boston Red Sox. The Yankees have won 27 World Series titles, more than any other team. The Cardinals are second with 11 championships.

>>> In 2019, the Minnesota Twins hit 307 home runs, the most ever by a team in a single season.

>>> The 1916 New York Giants won 26 games in a row. It's the longest winning streak in major-league history. The Baltimore Orioles set an AL record by losing their first 21 games in a row during the 1988 season.

>>> The New York Yankees have 24 players inducted into the Hall of Fame, the most in the AL. In the NL, the New York Giants come in first with 20 players.

>>> The Dodgers have lost 14 World Series, more than any other team in baseball. But they've also won six of them.

GLOSSARY

batting average: the rate of hits per times at bat

closer: a relief pitcher who specializes in finishing games

curse: a cause of harm or misery, often considered magical in nature

dynasty: a long period of dominance by a team, usually including multiple championships

earned run average (ERA): the rate of earned runs allowed per nine innings pitched

era: a long and distinct period

pennant: a league championship. The AL and NL pennant winners meet in the World Series.

rookie: a first-year player

segregate: separate by race

LEARN MORE

Baseball Reference
https://www.baseball-reference.com/

Fishman, Jon M. *Baseball's G.O.A.T.: Babe Ruth, Mike Trout, and More.*
Minneapolis: Lerner Publications, 2020.

The Official Site of Major League Baseball
https://www.mlb.com/

Scheff, Matt. *The World Series: Baseball's Fall Classic.* Minneapolis:
Lerner Publications, 2021.

Sports Illustrated Kids: Baseball
https://www.sikids.com/baseball

Weakland, Mark. *Baseball Records.* Mankato, MN: Black Rabbit
Books, 2021.

INDEX

American League (AL), 8, 14–15, 19, 23, 24–25, 27

American League Championship Series (ALCS), 9, 11, 15

Baltimore Orioles, 14–15

Chicago Cubs, 5, 16–17, 25

Chicago White Sox, 8–9

Cincinnati Reds, 5, 12–13, 15, 23

National League (NL), 4, 12, 17, 21

New York Yankees, 5, 11, 13, 15, 18–19, 21, 22–27

Philadelphia Athletics, 5, 24–25

playoffs, 9, 13, 17

postseason, 5, 9, 13, 15, 19

regular season, 5, 8–9, 11, 15, 16–17, 19, 21, 23, 26

Seattle Mariners, 5, 10–11

St. Louis Cardinals, 20–21

World Series, 5, 6, 9, 11, 13, 15, 16–17, 19, 21, 23, 25, 27

PHOTO ACKNOWLEDGMENTS

Image credits: Ezra Shaw/Getty Images, p. 1; Erik Drost/flickr (CC BY 2.0), p. 4; Photo File/Hulton Archive/Getty Images, pp. 6, 7; Stephen Green/Major League Baseball/Getty Images, p. 8; Rob Leiter/Major League Baseball/Getty Images, p. 9; Otto Greule Jr/Allsport/Getty Images, pp. 10, 11; Herb Scharfman/Sports Imagery/Getty Images, p. 12; Sporting News Archive/Getty Images, p. 13; Focus on Sport/Getty Images, pp. 14, 15; Gregory Shamus/Getty Images, p. 16; Rob Tringali/Major League Baseball/Getty Images, p. 17; David Seelig/Getty Images, p. 18; BOB ROSAT/AFP/Getty Images, p. 19; Bettmann/Getty Images, pp. 20, 21, 22, 23, 26, 27; AP Photo, pp. 24, 25; MH STOCK/Shutterstock.com, p. 28 (baseball glove). Design elements: ijaydesign99/Shutterstock.com; EFKS/Shutterstock.com; Vitalii Kozyrskyi/Shutterstock.com; RaiDztor/Shutterstock.com; MIKHAIL GRACHIKOV/Shutterstock.com; ESB Professional/Shutterstock.com; Roman Sotola/Shutterstock.com; MEandMO/Shutterstock.com.

Cover: Ezra Shaw/Getty Images. Design elements: Eugene Onischenko/Shutterstock.com; RaiDztor/Shutterstock.com; MIKHAIL GRACHIKOV/Shutterstock.com; ijaydesign99/Shutterstock.com.